To Maya, thanks for reminding me to always be passionately curious about the world and to never lose my sense of wonder.

Yes She Can LLC
Orlando, FL 32801
yesshecanllc@gmail.com

MAYA
THE ENGINEER

AMANDA GREEN

ILLUSTRATED BY: AFRA AMIN

EDITED BY: MADISON DIADDEZIO

Maya has an exciting week ahead of her of exploring and innovating. One day, her work is going to help a lot of people in many different ways!

On Monday, Maya is an

ARCHITECTURAL ENGINEER

who coordinates the construction of all of the

building systems.

Building systems that work well together keep the people inside safe, happy, and healthy.

As a
CIVIL ENGINEER

on Tuesday, Maya is testing the soil to plan a new irrigation system.

The irrigation plan will get water to the soil to help grow many crops to feed the community. Healthier soil will help remove bad gases from the air that cause climate change!

Wednesday comes around, and Maya is a

CHEMICAL ENGINEER

making the correct formulas for her new makeup

products.

She creates products that are gentle on people's skin, with ingredients that are better for the environment.

Then on Thursday, Maya is an

ELECTRICAL ENGINEER

designing new circuits and testing them.

These circuits will carry power to the lights
and machines in the building!

On Friday, Maya is redesigning a new car as a

MECHANICAL ENGINEER.

Her designs use clean energy and will help the car travel a longer distance before it needs to be recharged.

Saturday comes around, and Maya is looking up to the sky to imagine the flight path of the rocket she helped design as an

AEROSPACE ENGINEER.

Rockets can help expand space exploration to learn more about other planets in our galaxy.

On Sunday, Maya programs new computer software to help teach other people how to code as a

COMPUTER SCIENTIST.

Her software can teach young girls and boys how to be a computer scientist just like her!

It's finally the end of a long week for Maya. With all of the learning and exploring she's done, she has the problem solving skills to become any type of engineer she wants to be. With hard work and determination, she can change the world!

ABOUT THE AUTHOR

Amanda Green currently lives in Orlando, FL as a mechanical engineer designing heating and cooling systems in buildings. She graduated with her Master's Degree in Architectural Engineering from Penn State University. Amanda entered this field with the hopes of one day designing building systems that have less of an environmental impact. In school, she was involved in the Women in Engineering Program and has always had a passion for encouraging more girls to pursue STEM-related careers. She hopes that this book can inspire many young girls to want to be an engineer when they grow up.